The Flying Elephant

First published in 2009
by Wayland

Wayland
338 Euston Road
London NW1 3BH

Wayland Australia
Level 17/207 Kent Street
Sydney, NSW 2000

Series Editor: Louise John
Editor: Katie Powell
Cover design: Paul Cherrill
Design: D.R.ink
Consultant: Shirley Bickler

A CIP catalogue record for this book is available from the British Library.

ISBN 9780750257336

Printed in China

Wayland is a division of Hachette Children's Books,
an Hachette UK Company.
www.hachette.co.uk

The Flying Elephant

Written by Liss Norton
Illustrated by Emma McCann

WAYLAND

Fergus the Superfrog was playing hide and seek with his best friend, Doris the dragonfly, when he felt the ground shake.

Thump! Ka-bump!

He quickly pulled on his red suit,
his red helmet with a yellow stripe,
and his red rocket boots.

Then he and Doris flew off to find out what was going on.

A big elephant was stomping towards the pond.

"Who are you?" croaked Fergus.

“I’m Nora,” said the elephant. “I was on my way back to India to live in the wild. But I fell off the lorry.”

“Now I’ll have to walk all the way there,” said Nora, sighing a big sigh.

"You can't walk to India," explained Doris. "It's too far."

"I'll have to stay here then," said Nora.

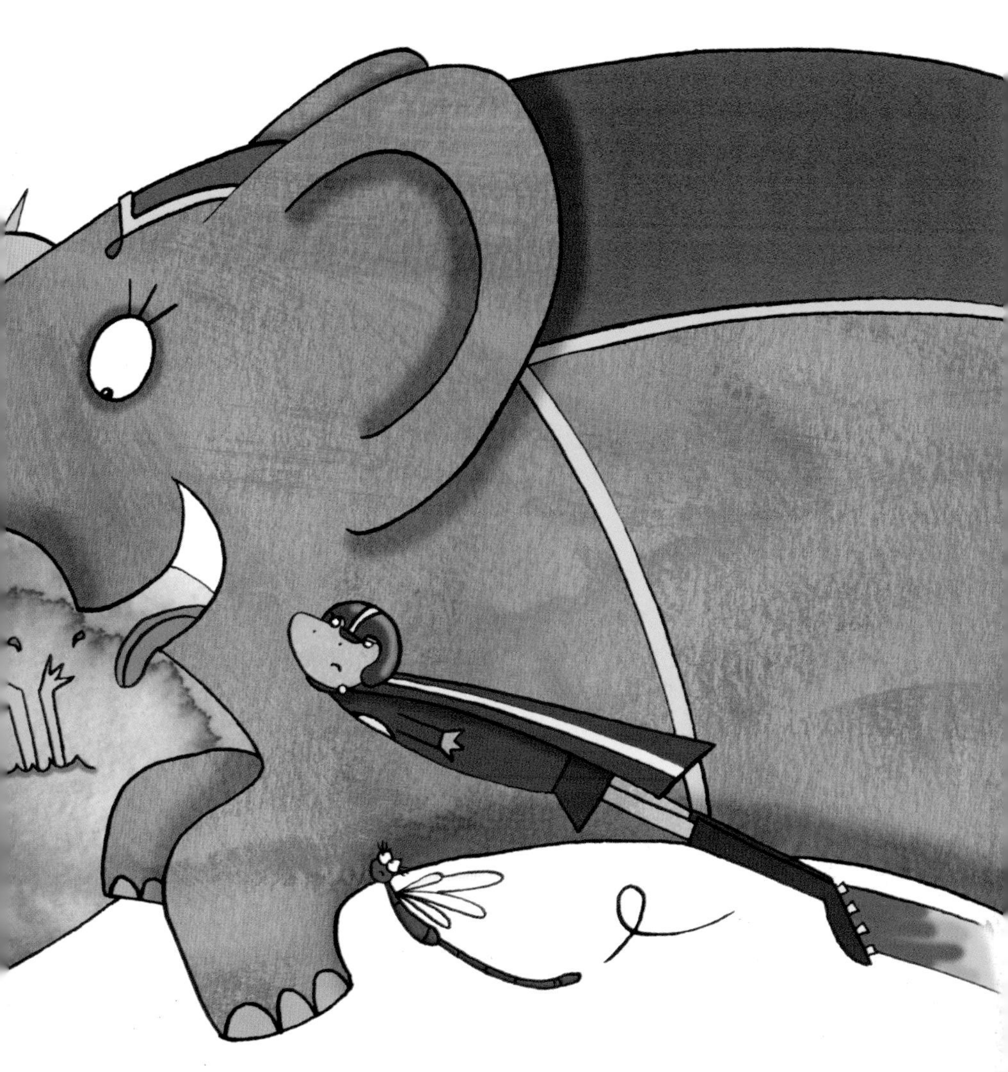

And, with that, she charged
towards the pond.

“I need a drink of water!”
she trumpeted.

Nora dipped her trunk in the pond...

...and began to suck up all the water.

“Stop!” shouted Fergus. “All my family live in that pond!”

Aunty Mabel held onto a rock to stop herself being sucked up. “Vernon’s gone up her trunk!” she croaked.

Doris grabbed a leaf and tickled Nora's trunk.

"Atishoo!" Nora sneezed, and all the water squirted back into the pond.

Fergus's cousin Vernon splashed out too.

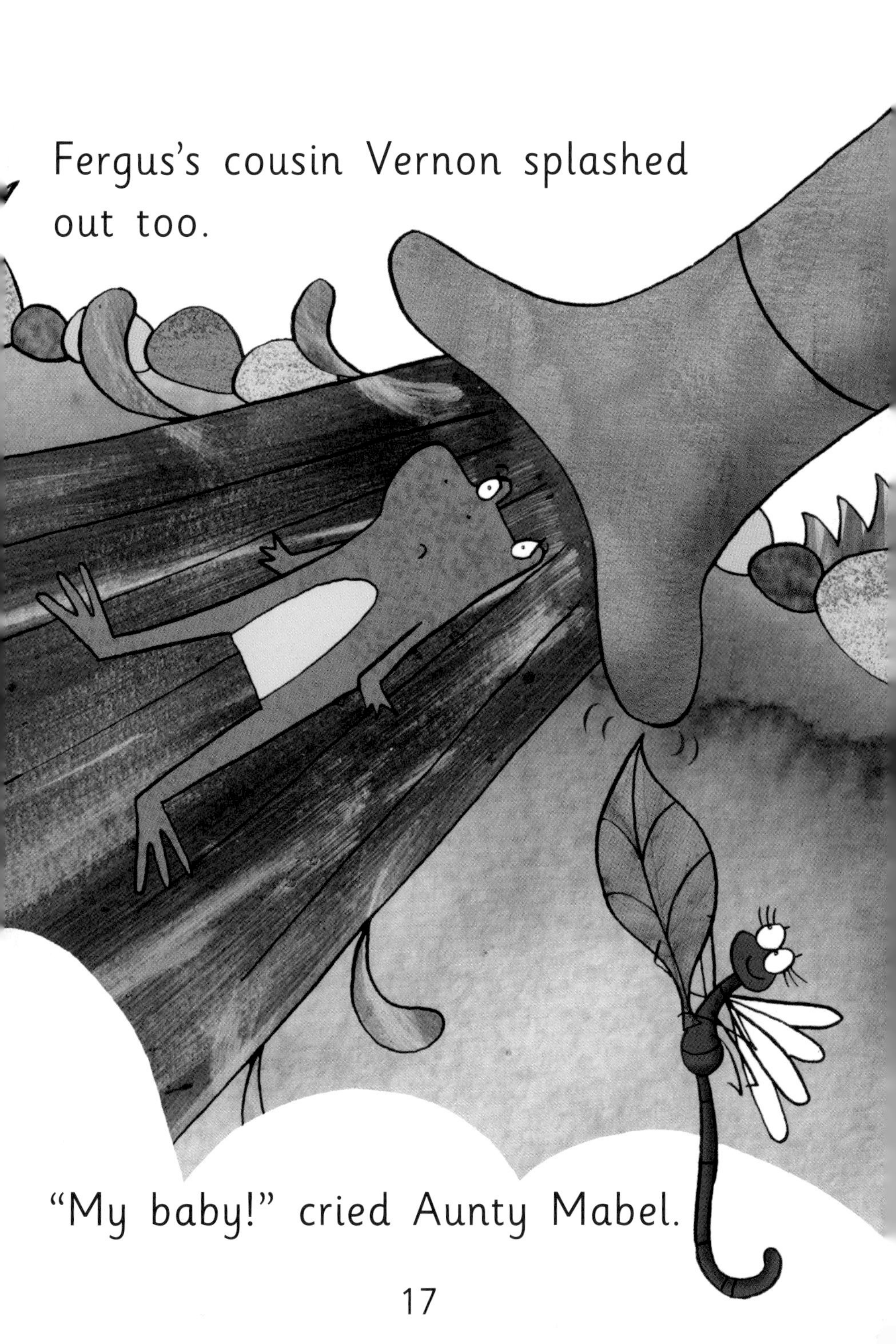

"My baby!" cried Aunty Mabel.

“The pond is our home,” said Fergus. “Just have a small drink, and then I’ll help you find that lorry.”

Nora dipped her trunk into the pond again. She sucked up a little bit of water and squirted it into her mouth.

"Time to go now," Doris said.

Fergus flew towards Nora and, using his Superfrog powers, he lifted her up into the air. Nora was very heavy.

“Wow!” shouted Nora, as they zoomed higher and higher. “I’m flying!”

“Keep your eyes peeled for that lorry, everyone,” Doris said.

“There’s a lorry,” said Nora, pointing. “And look, there’s another one.”

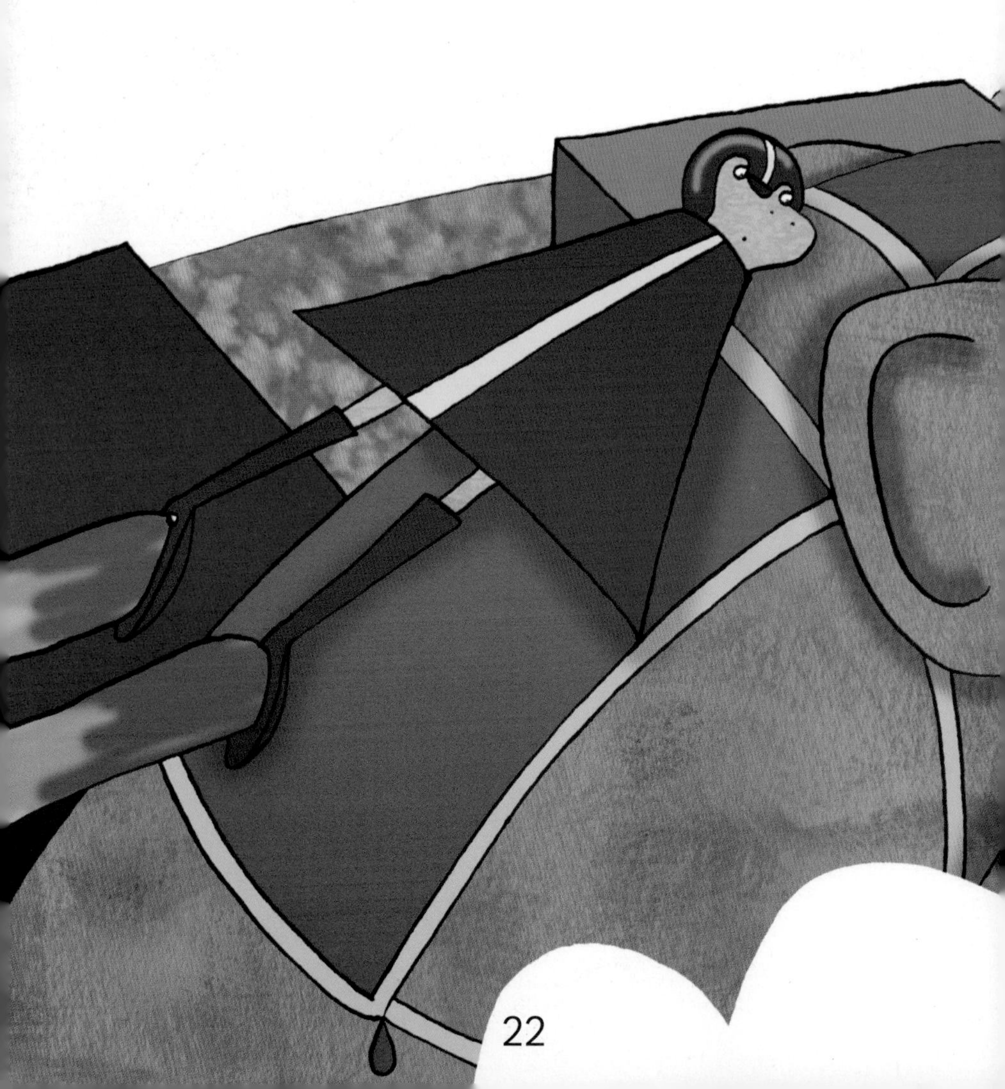

“The road is full of lorries,” said Doris. “We’ll never find the right one.”

Fergus flew on and on.
At last, they came to the sea.

"I'm getting tired," moaned Fergus.
"I can't fly any further."

Even though he was a Superfrog,
Fergus was still very small, and
Nora was an enormous elephant!

"Wait! There's the lorry on the back of that boat!" cried Nora. "I can see all my friends."

Fergus used the last of his Superfrog strength to reach the boat.

Fergus dropped Nora onto the lorry and landed in an exhausted heap next to her.

“Nora’s back!” trumpeted all the elephants. “Superfrog has saved the day!”

"I can't thank you both enough," said Nora. "Don't forget to come and visit me in India, will you?"

“We won’t forget,” laughed Doris.
“Fergus is so tired, he’ll need a holiday now!”

START READING is a series of highly enjoyable books for beginner readers. **The books have been carefully graded to match the Book Bands widely used in schools.** This enables readers to be sure they choose books that match their own reading ability.

Look out for the Band colour on the book in our Start Reading logo.

The Bands are:

Pink Band 1A & 1B

Red Band 2

Yellow Band 3

Blue Band 4

Green Band 5

Orange Band 6

Turquoise Band 7

Purple Band 8

Gold Band 9

START READING books can be read independently or shared with an adult. They promote the enjoyment of reading through satisfying stories supported by fun illustrations.

Liss Norton used to be a teacher. She now writes books, musicals and plays for children. She is keen on growing organic fruit and veg at her allotment, on her granddaughters, Maddie and Arabella, and on visiting castles. One day she hopes to find a secret passage...

Emma McCann is currently living a dual life. By day, she is a mild-mannered illustrator, but by night she becomes the masked crime-fighter and master cake-baker "Red Velvet". She hopes to be joined soon in her crime fighting/cake baking adventures by a small, dog-shaped partner.